The Pony and
the Bear

Do you love ponies? Be a Pony Pal!

Pony Pals

The Pony and the Bear

Jeanne Betancourt

illustrated by Vivien Kubbos

SCHOLASTIC INC.
New York Toronto London Auckland Sydney
Mexico City New Delhi Hong Kong

ISBN 0-439-06489-9

Text copyright © 1999 by Jeanne Betancourt.
Cover and text illustrations copyright © 1999 by Scholastic Australia.
All rights reserved.
Published by Scholastic Inc., 555 Broadway, New York, NY 10012,
by arrangement with Scholastic Australia Pty Limited.
PONY PALS, SCHOLASTIC and associated logos are trademarks and/or registered trademarks of Scholastic Inc.

12 11 10 9 8 7 6 5 4 3 2 1   9/9 0 1 2 3 4/0

Printed in Australia

First Scholastic printing, November 1999

Cover and text illustrations by Vivien Kubbos
Typeset in Bookman

Thank you to Jan White and Linda Brink for sharing their knowledge of wild animals, particularly black bears.

Contents

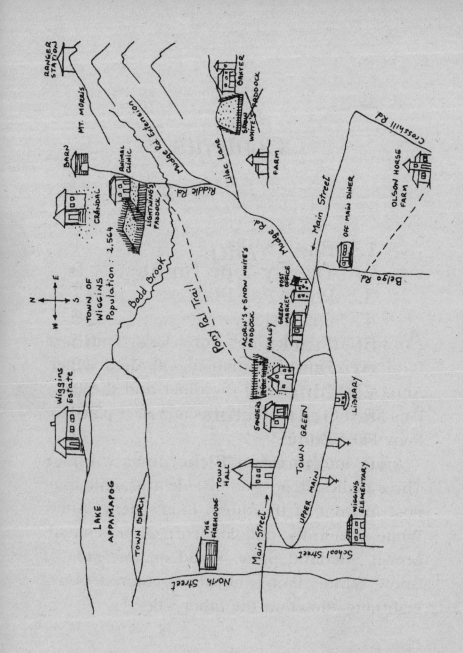

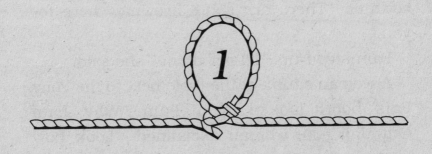

Big

Anna Harley and her Pony Pals, Pam and Lulu, were having lunch at Off-Main Diner. Anna's mother owned the diner and the Pony Pals loved to go there. It was a perfect place for Pony Pal Meetings.

Anna looked through the diner window. Three ponies stood side by side at the hitching post in front of the diner. Lulu's pony, Snow White, was in the middle. Acorn, Anna's small, brown Shetland pony, stood on one side of Snow White. Pam's chestnut-colored pony, Lightning, stood on the other side.

"Girls," Anna's mother called from the counter. "There are some brownies here for you."

Pam stood up. "I'll get them," she said.

A woman sitting at the table next to the Pony Pals booth looked up at Pam. "Why, Pam Crandall!" the woman exclaimed. "Look how you've grown! You're going to be as tall as your mother."

Pam smiled at the woman. "Thanks," she said.

Anna knew that the woman was right. Pam had grown a lot in the last year. Pam is the tallest of the Pony Pals, thought Anna. And I'm the shortest. Anna's mother was short, too. So was her father and her older sister and brother. Anna liked being short, except when everyone made such a big deal about being tall.

"Anna, look!" said Lulu. "Here comes Charlie Chase."

Through the window Anna saw Charlie Chase jump down from his pony, Moondance. He tied Moondance next to Snow White at the hitching post. The two ponies sniffed each other's face like old pony friends.

"Remember when Moondance and Snow White didn't get along?" said Lulu.

Anna remembered. She also remembered how much she used to like Charlie Chase. She had first met him at Mr. Olson's Horse Farm. Mr. Olson was Charlie's uncle and Charlie was staying at the farm for the summer. Charlie could do all sorts of western riding tricks and liked hanging out and riding with the Pony Pals. But lately Anna missed being just the three Pony Pals. She also thought that Charlie Chase was a show-off.

Pam came back to the Pony Pal booth, carrying a plate of brownies. She put it in the middle of the table and sat down next to Anna.

"Charlie's here," Lulu told Pam.

"Just in time for brownies," said Pam with a laugh.

Charlie came over to their booth and Lulu slid over to make room for him.

"Hey," Charlie said as he sat down.

"Have a brownie," said Pam as she pushed the plate in his direction.

"Thanks," he said.

"Have you been practicing your western riding tricks with Moondance today?" asked Lulu.

"Today I worked with Handsome," said Charlie.

"Handsome's so big!" exclaimed Pam.

"That's why I was riding him," Charlie told her. "My uncle said I'm getting too big for a pony and that I should start working with a horse."

"You're not going to ride Moondance anymore?" asked Anna.

"I'll use him for trail rides around here," said Charlie. "But when I go home I'll give him to my little brother. I'm getting myself a horse."

Why does he sound so happy? wondered Anna. I'd be so upset if I couldn't fit on Acorn anymore.

"What are you guys doing this afternoon?" asked Charlie.

"We haven't decided yet," answered Pam.

"Let's go on a really big trail ride," suggested Lulu.

Charlie laughed.

"What's so funny?" asked Anna.

"A big trail ride?" he teased. "You don't go on long trail rides around here. In the east you go out for a few hours. Out west, we ride for days at a time. That's a big trail ride."

"I see what you mean," said Lulu. "Everything is so big out west."

"That's right," agreed Charlie. "Big ranches, big spaces, big animals."

"What big animals?" asked Anna.

"Moose, mountain lions, grizzly bears," answered Charlie.

"We have black bears," said Lulu. "They're not dangerous like grizzly bears, but they're pretty big."

"Black bears in Wiggins?" asked Charlie as he reached for another brownie. "Have you ever seen one?"

"No," said Lulu. "But my father said there are some."

"I saw a grizzly bear back home once," said Charlie. "And I see moose all the time."

Lulu wanted to hear all about the big animals Charlie saw out west. Pam asked him about the big trail rides he went on. Anna didn't have any questions for Charlie Chase. She was sick of hearing about the big animals and the big trail rides and the big west.

While the others talked, Anna stared out the window. She saw Tommy Rand and Mike Lacey riding their bikes into the diner parking lot. Tommy and Mike were eighth grade bullies who were always teasing the Pony Pals. And they are *always* bragging, thought Anna. Just like Charlie Chase.

"Tommy and Mike are out front," Anna announced.

Lulu, Pam and Charlie looked out the window at the two boys speeding around the parking lot.

"Tommy has a new bike," said Lulu.

"Who are those guys?" asked Charlie.

"They go to our school," said Pam.

Charlie leaned over to get a better look out

the window. He made a whistling sound through his teeth. "Super mountain bike," he said. "I have a mountain bike back home. We go on these long rides."

In the wide open BIG spaces with the BIG animals, thought Anna.

Tommy and Mike skidded to a stop. Tommy held Mike's bike, while Mike took the new bike.

"Let's go out and see Tommy's new bike," suggested Anna.

"You hate Tommy," said Lulu. "Why do you want to see his bike?"

"It looks like a nice bike," said Anna.

While Pam and Lulu cleared the table, Anna went outside with Charlie. She hoped that BIG Tommy and BIG Mike would like BIG Charlie. Then maybe they would take him on a BIG bike ride . . . and leave the Pony Pals alone.

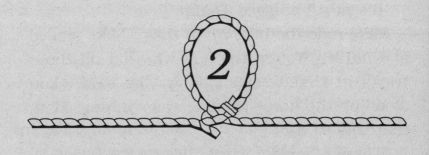

Twenty-four Hours

Tommy was leaning against a car, watching Mike ride the new bike around the parking lot. He saw Anna Harley and a stranger come out of the diner together.

"Hey, it's a Pony Pest," shouted Tommy.

"What did he call you?" Charlie asked Anna.

"He's just fooling around," said Anna. "Come on, I'll introduce you. Maybe he'll let you ride his bike."

Charlie and Anna walked over to Tommy. "Tommy, this is Charlie," said Anna. "Charlie, this is Tommy."

"Nice bike, Tom!" Charlie said enthusiastically.

"It's new," bragged Tommy.

Mike rode the bike up to them. Mike smiled at Charlie. "You're the guy who did all those tricks at that western show," he said. "You stood on the horse while it was running. Man, that was so cool."

"Thanks," said Charlie. "How's the bike?"

"Great!" exclaimed Mike. "Wish it was mine."

Tommy showed Charlie all the great things about his new bike. Charlie kept saying, "Wow!" and "Great!".

"You want to try it?" Tommy asked Charlie.

"Sure," said Charlie. "Thanks!"

Lulu and Pam came out of the diner and Anna ran over to meet them. The three friends stood on the steps of the diner watching Charlie ride Tommy's new bike.

"I think Charlie wants to hang out with Tommy and Mike," said Anna. "We might as well go."

As the Pony Pals walked towards the hitching post, Charlie whizzed past them on the bike.

"We're going to Anna's!" shouted Pam.

"Okay," Charlie called over his shoulder.

"See you later," called Lulu.

Anna didn't bother to say anything.

The Pony Pals unhitched their ponies and mounted them.

Riding home behind Lulu and Pam, Anna thought about her Pony Pals. Pam Crandal's father was a veterinarian and her mother was a riding teacher. Pam had been around horses all her life. She'd had her own pony for as long as she could remember. Anna thought that Pam knew more about horses and ponies than Charlie Chase.

Lulu's father studied and wrote about wild animals. Her mother had died when Lulu was little. After that, Lulu traveled all over the world with her father studying animals. Now Lulu lived in Wiggins with her grandmother, but her father kept going on his trips. Anna liked that Lulu didn't brag about the trips she'd been on, or all the things she knew about animals.

Anna thought that Pam and Lulu knew a lot of things that she didn't know. And they got better grades in school than she did. Pam and

Lulu loved reading and writing and liked going to school.

Anna was dyslexic, so reading and writing were hard for her. Pam and Lulu said Anna was a great artist. Anna loved doing art and knew that she drew good pictures. But at report card time she still felt terrible.

The Pony Pals were riding along Main Street when Mr. Sanders' big green van drove past them. He waved as he passed.

Lulu turned in the saddle and shouted to her friends, "My dad's home from Canada."

The girls put their ponies in the paddock behind Anna's house and ran over to Lulu's backyard. Mr. Sanders came out to meet them. He gave Lulu a big hug.

"Did you see lots of black bears, Dad?" asked Lulu.

"I did," answered her father. "And it was *very* interesting."

"How big were they?" asked Anna.

"I saw one that must have been five hundred pounds," answered Mr. Sanders.

"That's huge!" exclaimed Anna.

"I saw a lot of animals, big and small," Mr. Sanders told the girls. "I camped in one spot for a whole week and wrote down everything I observed. I took photographs, too. I'm calling my article 'A week in the woods of north-eastern Canada'."

"Did you ever see a black bear around here?" asked Pam.

"No," said Mr. Sanders. "There aren't that many in this region. Not many people have seen them up close."

"We're out in the woods a lot," said Lulu. "And we haven't seen one."

"If you do, let me know," said Mr. Sanders "I'd be very interested."

Mr. Sanders went into the house to unpack and the Pony Pals went back to the Harley paddock.

They sat on the fence and watched their ponies.

"We should do what my father did," suggested Lulu.

"Go to Canada?" asked Anna.

"No," replied Lulu. "But we could camp out

near Wiggins and write down everything we see."

"That'd be so much fun," said Pam.

"For a whole week?" asked Anna.

"We could do it for twenty-four hours," said Lulu. "But we'd write down everything and take pictures."

Anna thought about how she didn't like to write that much. But she liked camping.

"Let's take turns staying up all night," said Pam. "That way we won't miss anything."

"Perfect," said Lulu. "Let's do it tomorrow."

"We'll bring binoculars," suggested Lulu. "And my camera."

"And our Pony Pal notebooks," added Pam.

"I could bring my tape recorder," suggested Anna. "That way we can record some of the sounds we hear."

"We have to plan the food we'll bring," said Lulu.

"We can pack everything this afternoon," said Pam. "Then let's have a barn sleepover at my place. That way we can start out early tomorrow morning."

15

Lulu jumped down from the fence. "Maybe we could write an article, too," she said. "For a kids' magazine."

"That's a great idea!" exclaimed Pam.

Anna didn't think writing an article was such a great idea. It sounded too hard.

"Let's stay at that lean-to near Mount Morris," suggested Lulu. "I bet there'll be bears around there."

"I really want to see one," said Pam. "It would be so exciting."

Anna imagined seeing a five-hundred-pound bear in the woods. Just the idea terrified her. But Lulu and Pam weren't afraid. They thought seeing a huge bear would be exciting. Everyone is braver than me, thought Anna.

Suddenly Acorn ran towards the fence and whinnied excitedly. Anna turned around and saw Charlie riding Moondance towards them.

Anna hoped that Lulu and Pam wouldn't invite Charlie to go on the camping trip with them.

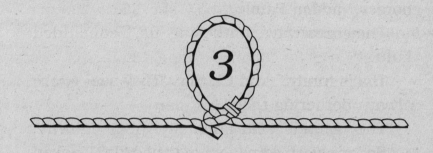

Pony Pal Plan

Pam and Lulu ran up the Harley driveway to meet Charlie and Moondance. Anna took her time.

Charlie halted his pony and looked down at Lulu and Pam. "Tom and Mike are cool," he said. "Tom let me ride his bike and everything."

Anna noticed that Charlie wasn't getting off Moondance. She hoped that meant he wasn't staying.

"Those guys are always mean to us," said Lulu.

"And they don't know anything about horses," added Pam.

"They're always bothering us," concluded Lulu.

"That's funny," said Charlie. "They said you're always bothering them."

"They would," said Lulu.

"So are you going on a trail ride?" asked Charlie.

Lulu shook her head. "We're planning an overnight camping trip instead."

"We're leaving early tomorrow morning," said Pam.

"We're looking for animals," added Lulu. "And writing down everything we see."

"Out west I camped out three nights," Charlie said. "Me and two other cowboys. We were driving this big herd of cattle. I saw a grizzly bear on that trip and more moose than I could count."

"You already told us about the bear," Anna reminded him. "Anyway, this trip is a Pony Pal Project." She hoped that Charlie would get the hint that he wasn't invited.

18

"Sorry, but I can't go with you," Charlie said. "I told Tom and Mike I'd ride mountain bikes with them tomorrow. Tom's lending me his old bike. They go on a lot of the trails I've been riding with you guys."

"We know," said Anna. "They're not too smart about using the woods."

"They make fires," said Lulu.

"And set traps to catch animals," added Pam.

"Lots of people have camp fires," said Charlie. "And trapping animals is legal."

I can't believe he's defending Tommy and Mike, thought Anna. She was going to explain to Charlie that camp fires were not allowed in the woods around Wiggins. And you could only trap in some places, if you had a special permit. But Charlie was already turning Moonstone around to leave.

"Gotta go," he called to the Pony Pals. "I'm meeting Tom and Mike at my uncle's. Tom wants to see me do riding tricks."

"Bye," said Pam.

Charlie rode back towards Main Street.

"Good riddance," mumbled Anna.

19

"He actually likes Tommy and Mike," said Pam.

"That is *so* weird," added Lulu.

The three girls walked back to the paddock.

"Charlie doesn't know how awful they can be," said Pam.

"Maybe he's just as awful as they are," said Anna. "Maybe that's why he wants to hang out with them."

"I don't think Charlie is awful," said Lulu defensively.

"Charlie's older than us and he's a boy," explained Pam. "So he probably just wants to hang out with boys his own age."

"Good," said Anna. "Let's forget about him and get ready for our camping trip."

The Pony Pals went over to Lulu's house and sat around the kitchen table. First, they made a menu for the meals they would eat on their trip.

"We'll eat breakfast before we leave," said Pam. "So the first meal we need to plan is lunch."

In a little while the girls had a menu. Pam

read it out loud to be sure they all agreed that it was good.

MENU FOR TWENTY-FOUR-HOUR
NATURE WATCH

LUNCH
peanut butter and jelly sandwiches
apples
cookies
juice

DINNER
ham and cheese sandwiches
brownies

BREAKFAST
juice
cereal
bananas

SNACKS
juice
trail mix
candy

"Perfect," said Lulu. "Now let's figure out what food we already have in our houses. Then we'll buy the rest at the grocery store."

An hour later the Pony Pals had finished

21

their shopping and were ready to go to Pam's for the sleepover. They saddled up their ponies and rode them onto Pony Pal Trail. The mile-and-a-half woodland trail connected the Harley paddock to the Crandals' property.

Anna took the lead. Pony Pal Trail was one of her favorite places to ride. A lot of Pony Pal adventures had started there. She remembered some of those adventures as they rode along.

When the three girls galloped off Pony Pal Trail and raced across the Crandals' big field, Anna and Acorn kept the lead. Anna slowed Acorn down when they came to the barn.

"Good pony," she told Acorn as she slid off the saddle. She led Acorn to a shady spot to take off his tack and wipe him down. I wouldn't trade Acorn for a horse, she thought. He's small and strong and the best pony in the world. Who says big is better? Just dumb people like Charlie Chase.

"Let's do the schedule for the night watch next," suggested Pam.

"Okay," agreed Lulu.

A few minutes later the girls were sitting at

a haybale table in the hayloft. Pam took her pad and a pen out of her backpack.

"Let's stay up until ten o'clock," suggested Lulu. "Then take turns staying awake from ten o'clock at night until six the next morning."

"That's eight hours for us to split up three ways," said Pam. She thought for a few seconds. "If we all get up at five-thirty, then we can do two-and-a-half hours each. That'll work out perfectly."

Anna was amazed at how fast Pam did math. A few minutes later the schedule was ready.

NIGHT WATCH FOR TWENTY-FOUR-HOUR

NATURE STUDY

10.00p.m.-12.30am Pam

12.30a.m.-3.00a.m. Lulu

3.00a.m.-5.30a.m. Anna

"I hope I don't fall asleep while I'm supposed to watch," said Pam.

"Eat trail mix and candy while you're on

duty," suggested Lulu. "That will help you stay awake."

The girls spent the rest of the day preparing for their twenty-four-hour nature study. That night they ate dinner with Pam's family, did the dishes and then went back to the barn. Next, they laid out their three sleeping bags side by side on the floor of the hayloft. Then they went outside to say goodnight to their ponies.

At nine-thirty the three girls were in their sleeping bags ready to go to sleep.

Anna lay looking at the starlit sky through the loft window. She imagined herself on the night watch. Pam and Lulu would be asleep in the lean-to. She'd be awake looking out for wild animals, alone. What if she saw a bear?

Lulu and her father said black bears weren't dangerous. But Anna thought that anything that weighs five hundred pounds had to be dangerous. She wished she could feel brave like Pam and Lulu. But she didn't.

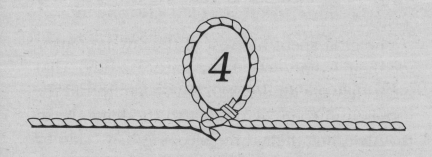

Grr-rr!

By nine o'clock the next morning the Pony Pals were on their camping trip. Pam took the lead on the narrow trail through the woods. When she suddenly halted Lightning, Anna and Lulu stopped behind her.

Pam turned in the saddle and whispered, "I just saw a red fox. It ran across the trail."

"I saw it, too," added Lulu excitedly.

"I didn't," mumbled Anna.

Pam made a quick entry in her notebook, then they rode on.

An hour later, the Pony Pals reached their

camp site near Mt. Morris. A one-sided lean-to was at the edge of a small clearing next to Badd Brook. A small corral and hitching post were near the lean-to.

The girls took the sleeping bags and saddle bags off the ponies and placed them on the lean-to floor. Next, they removed the ponies' bridles and saddles, wiped the ponies down and led them to the brook for a drink.

By the time the ponies were safely grazing in the corral, the Pony Pals were hungry. They sat on rocks beside the brook and passed around sandwiches.

"I want to hike around here this afternoon," said Lulu. "We could look for signs of animals— like tracks, nests and scat."

"What's scat?" asked Anna.

"Animal droppings," answered Lulu. "You know—poop."

"Two of us can do that," suggested Pam, "while the other one stays here to watch the ponies."

"And records the animal life," added Lulu.

27

"That's important. We need to know what animals come around here during the day."

"What do you want to do, Anna?" asked Pam. "Stay here or go with Lulu?"

Anna didn't want to be left alone at the camp site. But she didn't want her friends to know she was afraid. "I don't care," she said. "What do you want to do, Pam?"

"I want to go with Lulu," said Pam.

"Okay," said Anna. "I'll stay here."

After the three girls finished eating, Lulu and Pam prepared for their hike.

They put water bottles in their backpacks. Lulu put her camera in her pocket and Pam had a pair of binoculars. They both took their notebooks and pens.

"Don't forget to write down everything you see here," Lulu told Anna. "Use your binoculars."

"Sound the SOS with your whistle if you need us to come back," added Pam.

"And you whistle if you need me," Anna reminded her friends.

Lulu looked at her watch. "We'll come back

here at two o'clock. Then we'll decide what to do next."

Anna watched Pam and Lulu go into the thick woods. She walked over to a fallen tree trunk and sat down to observe the animal life. She took out her binoculars and peered up into the trees. Maybe I'll see some interesting birds, she thought. I could draw pictures. We can look them up later in Lulu's bird book.

Anna scanned the tree tops with the binoculars for a long time. But she didn't see any birds. She didn't hear any either. There wasn't a sound in the woods.

Looking down, she noticed a row of ants going in and out of the log she was sitting on. She looked at them through the binoculars. The ants looked huge, like characters in a horror film.

Frightened, Anna jumped up from the log and ran over to the lean-to. She sat on her rolled-up sleeping bag which was more comfortable than a log and less scary. A squirrel ran up the tree in front of the lean-to and jumped from branch to branch. Anna was writing about the squirrel in her notebook, when a second squirrel joined in the fun.

A little later Anna heard a knocking noise. Tap-tap-tap. Tap-tap-tap. That's a woodpecker, she thought. She left the lean-to and searched the trees for the woodpecker. When she finally spotted it, she drew a little picture and made notes.

Woodpecker. Red.

Next, Anna went over to the corral to check on the ponies. When Acorn saw her, he ran over. Anna rested her cheek against his smooth neck. "It was silly of me to be afraid of being

alone," she told her pony. "Besides, I'm not alone if you're here."

Suddenly, Snow White startled and whinnied nervously. Anna looked around. She didn't see any snakes in the corral or anything else that might startle a pony. She listened carefully, but didn't hear anything. Anna remembered that ponies have better hearing than people. What had startled Snow White?

Anna walked out of the corral and took a few steps towards the woods. She stopped and listened again. This time she heard something. At first the sound was soft, but then it became closer and louder.

"Grr-rr, grr-rr."

What kind of animal would make a noise like that? A fox or coyote would bark or howl. This sound was more like a growl. Was it a bear?

"Grr-rr! Grr-rr."

The growls were louder and closer now. Anna stepped back into the corral and raised the whistle to her lips to blow the SOS signal for Pam and Lulu. She stopped before she blew.

Lulu's father said black bears weren't dangerous.

Lightning startled and looked around nervously. "It's okay," Anna whispered to the frightened pony.

There was rustling in a bush near the lean-to. Was the bear behind that bush? Even Acorn, the bravest of the ponies, was acting spooked. He snorted and pawed the ground. Anna was too frightened to write down anything. She thought of getting the tape recorder out of her backpack. But that was in the lean-to. I can't leave the ponies alone, she thought. Not with a ferocious-sounding animal nearby.

Another bush, on the other side of the lean-to, rustled. Were there two bears? wondered Anna. Or even three? Will they attack from all sides? She had to protect the ponies and herself. Then she thought she heard a giggle.

Bears don't giggle, thought Anna. But Lulu and Pam do! That's it, she thought. Pam and Lulu are playing a joke on me.

"Pam and Lulu, that is *not* funny!" Anna

shouted towards the bushes. "You scared the ponies."

But Pam and Lulu didn't answer or come out of the bushes. There were no more giggles either. Had she imagined the giggles? Was it just another strange sound that bears made?

For a few seconds all that Anna heard was the pounding of her heart. Then came another low, fierce growl.

Anna raised her whistle to her lips and blew out the SOS.

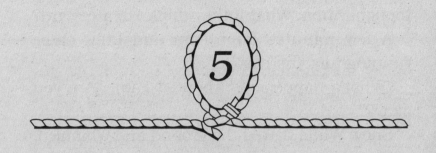

Tracks

Anna blew the SOS signal again. She stood still and listened for an answer to her call for help. A single whistle blast from deep in the woods answered her. Lulu and Pam had heard the SOS.

There was more rustling in the bushes. Anna was still frightened, but she knew that her friends were on their way to help her.

Anna waited near the corral while she watched the bushes and listened for more wild animal sounds. The bushes didn't move and there weren't any more scary noises.

What if Pam and Lulu don't believe me? thought Anna. What if they think I'm a coward?

A few minutes later Pam and Lulu came running into the clearing.

"What's happened?" shouted Pam. "Are you okay?"

Snow White pawed the ground and whinnied.

"Did something happen to Snow White?" asked Lulu.

"She's okay," said Anna. "We're all okay." She pointed to the bushes. "But there were some weird sounds in those bushes. I mean really scary. Like, Grr-rr. Grr-rr. It spooked the ponies—even Acorn. And me, too. I think it was a big animal, like a bear."

"What did it look like?" asked Pam.

"I didn't see it," answered Anna. "I just heard it. And the bushes moved. I think my SOS scared whatever it was away. I heard two of them. There could have been a whole bunch."

"I'm glad you called us," said Lulu.

"You did the right thing," agreed Pam.

"Let's go and look behind the bushes," suggested Lulu. "But be careful where you step.

We don't want to mess up any clues, like tracks in the dirt."

Pam and Anna followed Lulu to the other side of the bushes. Lulu stopped and bent over. "There are some tracks here," she said.

"Are they bear tracks?" asked Anna.

Lulu shook her head and pointed at the earth in front of her. "Look," she said.

Anna and Pam squatted and looked where Lulu was pointing. Anna saw long, even marks in the ground.

"It looks like bicycle tracks," said Pam.

"From a mountain bike," said Lulu. "A wild animal was here all right. A wild animal with the initials T.R."

"Tommy Rand," said Pam. "Which means Mike was probably with him." She looked up at Anna. "They were trying to scare you."

"I bet Charlie was here, too," said Anna.

"Charlie wouldn't play a mean joke like that," said Pam.

"He's the only one who knew where we were camping today," Anna reminded her.

"*And* where we were going," added Lulu. "He

said he was biking with Tommy and Mike today."

"I hate those guys!" said Anna. "That was such a mean thing to do."

Pam took out her notebook and wrote something. When she finished she held it up for Anna and Lulu to read:

Do you think they're still here?

Anna shrugged her shoulders that she didn't know. Were the boys still in the woods? She wondered. Were they still spying on the Pony Pals?

Lulu took the notebook from Pam and wrote:

Let's follow the tracks. Don't make a sound.

Pam took her notebook back and wrote:

I'll stay with the ponies.

Anna was glad that she didn't have to stay at the camp site alone again. Pam turned back towards the corral. "Anna, Lulu," she said in a loud voice to the air around her. "Let's go back to our camp site and check on the ponies."

Lulu and Anna exchanged a smile. Pam was pretending that all three of them were going back to the camp site. That way, if the boys were nearby, they wouldn't know they were being followed.

"Okay, Pam," shouted Anna. "I'm coming."

"Me, too," added Lulu.

Anna and Lulu turned and walked through the woods along the narrow trail that led away from their camp site. They looked for clues of which way the boys had gone. Lulu pointed to small tree branches that might have broken off when a kid on a bike rushed past. Anna found more tire tracks. A few feet later, she spotted a bright blue-and-red candy wrapper. She stuck it in her pocket. It was just like Tommy and Mike to litter. Or Charlie.

Finally, the two girls came out on the wider trail that led out of the woods. They listened carefully, but didn't hear any shouting, talking or laughing.

"I think they've gone all the way back to town," Lulu whispered.

"Now that they've had their fun," said Anna. "But I bet they'll come back and bother us some more."

"We just don't know when," said Lulu.

"We can't let them ruin our nature study," said Anna.

"Let's be very quiet going back to the camp site," suggested Lulu. "Maybe we'll see some animals."

"Good idea," agreed Anna.

On the walk back to the camp site, Anna and Lulu saw two rabbits, ten squirrels, turkey feathers, and lots of deer scat and deer tracks.

When they reached the camp site, Pam was sitting on the edge of the lean-to looking through her binoculars. Her open notebook was on her lap.

"I've been watching for birds and squirrels," Pam told Lulu and Anna. "I'm not going to let those guys ruin our nature study."

"That's what we decided," said Anna.

"They've left," said Lulu. "We followed their trail almost all the way to Riddle Road."

"Do you really think Charlie was with them?" asked Pam.

"We saw three separate tire tracks in one place," said Lulu. "So there were three of them."

"Three of them and three of us," said Anna.

The Pony Pals looked at one another. Anna knew Pam and Lulu were thinking the same thing that she was thinking. What would Tommy, Mike and Charlie do next to ruin their nature study?

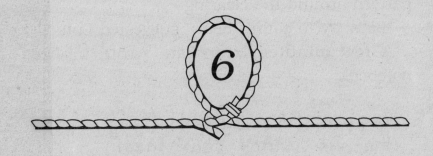

Snacks

The Pony Pals ate their supper under the pine trees at the edge of the clearing. From there they had a good view of the lean-to, the ponies and Badd Brook.

"Tommy and his gang won't trick us again," Lulu vowed.

At dusk a large deer and two spotted fawns came to the brook for a drink.

"I bet the fawns are twins," said Lulu as she made an entry in her notebook. "Deer have twins a lot."

Half an hour later, bats flew in a zigzag pattern around the clearing.

"Let's try to count them," suggested Lulu.

A few minutes later Pam wrote in her notebook:

8.30 p.m. So many bats flying around that we couldn't count them.

When the full moon rose over the treetops, the Pony Pals went back to the lean-to. They sat on their sleeping bags and talked about the animals they'd seen so far.

At ten o'clock, Lulu and Anna went to sleep and Pam began her watch.

As Anna was falling asleep, she wondered what she would see during her watch. Would she be afraid when she was the only one awake?

The next thing Anna knew, someone was whispering her name and gently poking her through the sleeping bag. Anna opened her eyes and saw Lulu leaning over her.

"Anna, it's your turn," Lulu whispered.

"Okay," Anna whispered back.

Anna pulled herself out of her sleeping bag, while Lulu slipped into hers.

"Did you see anything?" Anna asked.

"Three flying squirrels," said Lulu in a hushed voice. "And a raccoon. It left when it didn't find our food."

Anna looked up at the saddle bag of food hanging from a tree branch. She was glad it was in a safe place.

By the time Anna had put on her boots, Lulu was sound asleep.

Anna slung the backpack over her shoulder and left the lean-to. She walked over to the tree stump and sat down. The only animals Anna saw were the ponies; they were sleeping standing up. Snow White glowed in the moonlight.

Anna listened carefully. The woods were completely silent. She wished that Acorn was awake, then her night watch wouldn't be so lonely. She took a carton of juice out of her backpack. This will help keep me awake, she thought. I'll save the chocolate chip cookies for later.

A rustle in the trees above Anna startled her. She was wondering what made the noise, when she heard the 'whoo-who-whoo' of an owl. Another owl, deep in the woods, answered the first owl's call.

Anna opened her notebook and wrote by the light of the full moon.

Owl in trees near camp.
3.35 a.m. Other Owl in
woods answers.

Anna was closing her notebook when something flew out of a tree. She watched it sail through the air and land on another tree. The animal was about the size of a squirrel and had large eyes that shone in the night. It was too big to be a bat and didn't flap its wings the way bats did. Anna decided it was a flying squirrel.

She wrote the flying squirrel sighting in her notebook.

There was no more animal activity for a long while. Anna's eyes felt heavy and she wanted to go back to sleep. I have to stay awake, she told herself. She drank more juice and ate one of the chocolate chip cookies. When she finished eating she had to go to the bathroom. I'm only going to be gone for a few minutes, Anna thought, so I might as well leave my backpack here. She went into the woods next to the corral.

A minute later, Anna heard someone or something moving in the clearing behind her. She froze with fear. Who or what was in the clearing? Had Pam or Lulu woken up? Was it a wild animal? Or were the boys playing another trick on her?

Anna stood up and turned around. What she saw made her heart stop beating. Someone or something very big was tearing at her backpack. Anna couldn't tell if it was a person or a wild animal. She took a step forward to get a better view. It was a big black bear!

Anna quickly checked the corral beside her. Snow White and Lightning were still sleeping. But Acorn was waking up. Anna knew that if Acorn saw the bear he would whinny and scare it away. Even though Anna was afraid, she didn't want the bear to leave. She wanted to observe and draw it.

Anna silently slipped into the corral and went over to Acorn. Acorn sniffed the air and looked over his shoulder. He saw the bear, too. Anna rubbed her pony's cheeks and looked into his eyes. Acorn, please don't make any noise, she prayed.

Acorn nodded as if he understood. Then he looked back at the bear again, but he didn't make a sound.

Anna took out her notebook and began a drawing of the bear. It was standing on its hind legs while it tried to open her backpack. When the backpack ripped open, the bear dug out the chocolate chip cookie and stuffed it in its mouth. Next the bear found Anna's chocolate bar, which it ate with the wrapper still on it

Lulu told Anna and Pam that bears had a sweet tooth. Here was the evidence!

Anna was wondering what the bear would do next, when she heard a pony moving in the corral. Snow White was awake and had noticed the bear. She nickered fearfully.

The bear made a loud, fierce blowing sound as it bounded towards the corral. Lightning woke up, too. Acorn pawed the ground and Snow White whinnied again. Anna looked helplessly from the confused ponies to the attacking bear. What could she do to protect the ponies?

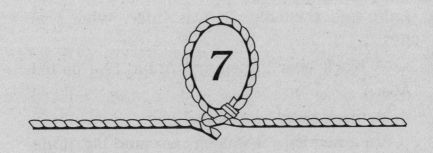

Clues

The bear clacked its teeth threateningly at Anna and the ponies. Snow White was backing up to jump over the corral fence to escape from the bear. The bear blew one more loud noise, then it turned around and ran on all fours into the woods.

The noisy ponies and bear woke up Lulu and Pam. They jumped out of their sleeping bags and ran over to the frightened ponies in the corral.

"What happened?" Pam shouted, climbing into the corral.

"I saw something running into the woods!" Lulu said excitedly. "It was huge. What was it?"

"A black bear," answered Anna. She patted Acorn.

"A black bear!" exclaimed Pam. "Really?"

Anna nodded. "It was so close and big. It ate stuff out of my backpack."

"You must have been so scared!" exclaimed Pam.

"I was mostly afraid Acorn would scare it away," Anna told them. "I wanted it to stay so I could do a drawing. But Acorn was perfect. He knew I wanted him to stay quiet and he did."

"That's amazing," said Pam. "Acorn really understands you."

"But that bear seemed really dangerous," said Anna. "It was making an awful blowing noise and ran towards the corral."

"It was bluffing," Lulu told Anna. "My dad says black bears do that. They're just trying to scare you. But it wouldn't attack or anything."

"Well, it scared me," admitted Anna.

"And you did a drawing?" asked Lulu. "In the dark?"

Anna nodded. "I had the moonlight," explained Anna. "But I have to work on it some more in the daytime."

"I wish you'd taken a photo, too," said Pam.

"The flash would have scared it away," said Anna.

"Good point," agreed Lulu.

"Let's go get your backpack," suggested Pam. "And see what damage it did."

Lulu put up a hand to stop Pam. "It's still pretty dark out. We might mess up any evidence, like bear tracks," she said. "In the daytime we can do a thorough investigation of the site without destroying evidence. We'll get the backpack then."

"Good idea," agreed Pam.

The girls went back to the lean-to. Anna told Pam and Lulu everything she could remember about the bear.

"My father is going to be so excited that you actually saw a bear," Lulu told Anna.

Pam looked at her watch. "It's four o'clock," she said.

"I have another hour-and-a-half to watch," said Anna. "You guys should get some more sleep. You've already watched."

"I can stay up with you, Anna," said Pam. "If you're afraid."

"I'm not afraid," said Anna confidently.

Pam and Lulu went back into their sleeping bags.

Anna sat on the edge of the lean-to platform and turned to a new page in her notebook. She was ready to draw and write about any other animals or birds that visited their camping site.

For a while there were no more visitors. But at dawn, three deer came to the brook for water. Anna did a drawing of them. She also drew two squirrels chasing one another around in a big pine tree near the lean-to. Then she worked on her drawing of the bear. A flock of crows flew into the clearing and walked around, cawing.

The crows made so much noise they woke up Pam and Lulu. It was six o'clock in the morning.

"Why didn't you wake us up at five-thirty?" asked Lulu. "That was the schedule."

"I sort of lost track of time," explained Anna. "I was busy drawing."

"Let's go over to the stump," suggested Lulu. "It's light enough to look for bear tracks now."

The three girls went over to the tree stump. Anna picked up her backpack. It had two tears in it, but the zipper still worked.

"I'm going to sew it," said Anna. "I want to always keep this backpack."

"You should name it The Bear," suggested Pam.

Anna laughed. "I will," she agreed.

Lulu and Pam studied the area around the tree stump.

"There's a perfect bear track in the mud right next to the stump," said Lulu. "Can you draw it, Anna?"

"Sure," agreed Anna.

Anna drew the bear track while Pam and Lulu got their breakfast out of the tree.

The three girls sat at the edge of the lean-to to eat their breakfast.

"I wish I'd seen the bear," said Pam.

"It was pretty exciting," Anna told her. "At first I thought Tommy and his gang were sneaking around here."

"I can't believe Charlie is hanging out with those guys," said Pam.

"He probably thought that we'd all be friends," said Lulu. "The six of us."

"He doesn't know all the mean things Mike and Tommy do," said Pam.

"We tried to tell him," said Anna. "He didn't listen to us." She handed Pam a box of cereal and the milk.

"I can't believe that he tried to scare you, too," added Pam.

"I can," said Anna. "He was showing off to

57

Mike and Tommy. He didn't care about ruining our nature watch."

"We used to have so much fun with Charlie," said Pam sadly.

"Used to," said Anna. "But no more. Now he's on their side."

"Maybe he thought it was a joke," suggested Lulu.

"Some joke!" Anna exclaimed. "He should have known better. Especially when there are ponies around. Snow White could have run away again."

Lulu put a finger to her lips. "Let's not talk so loud," she whispered. "We're still doing the nature watch. Maybe the bear will come back."

Lulu rolled up their sleeping bags, Anna put away the food and Pam fed the ponies. They were all keeping an eye out for animals and birds. Anna was walking between the lean-to and the corral when Acorn suddenly nickered. Anna stopped where she was and listened. Lulu and Pam froze in place, too.

Something was coming through the woods towards the camp site . . . something large.

Jelly Donuts

Acorn nickered again. This time a pony's whinny answered Acorn's call.

"It must be someone out trail riding," said Lulu.

"And they're coming this way," added Pam.

Just then Charlie Chase rode Moondance out of the woods and into the camp site. He waved and galloped up to Pam.

"Hi," Charlie said in a friendly voice.

"Hi," replied Pam in a not-very-friendly voice.

Lulu and Anna walked over to them.

"What are you doing here?" Lulu asked Charlie.

Anna didn't say anything.

"I came to see how your nature watch is going," Charlie said as he jumped down from Moondance. "I brought some fresh donuts. Can I put Moondance in the corral with your ponies?"

The Pony Pals exchanged a glance. Charlie was acting as if he hadn't played a prank on them the day before . . . as if nothing had happened.

Anna ran a hand gently along Moondance's smooth, sweaty neck. She was angry at Charlie, but not at his pony.

"Moondance is probably thirsty," said Anna. "He can have a drink from the brook."

"Good idea," said Charlie.

The three girls walked with Charlie and Moondance towards the brook.

"Where are your buddies, Tommy Rat and Mike Lousy?" Anna asked angrily. "Hiding in the bushes?"

"I don't know where they are," said Charlie.

"We know you came here with them yesterday," said Pam. "And that you tried to scare Anna."

"You almost ruined our nature watch," added Lulu.

"How do you know I was with them?" asked Charlie. "How do you know it was them in the first place?"

Lulu told Charlie how she identified three different sets of bike tracks in the mud.

"Besides, it's just the sort of stupid thing Tommy and Mike would do," added Anna.

"It was just a joke," said Charlie.

"Not funny," Anna grumbled.

"They aren't that much fun to hang out with," said Charlie. "I wish I'd been on the nature watch instead."

Moondance finished drinking and walked over to the corral with Charlie and the girls. Acorn ran over to meet Moondance.

Anna opened the gate for the pony. Charlie took a paper bag out of his saddle bag. "Sugar donuts and jelly donuts," he said.

"Jelly donuts are my favorites," said Lulu happily.

They were Anna's favorites, too, but she didn't say so.

The three girls and Charlie went to the lean-to to eat the donuts.

"Did you really stay awake all night?" asked Charlie.

"Yup," said Lulu. "It was exciting." She winked at Anna. "Wasn't it, Anna?"

"Yup," said Anna. She couldn't help smiling.

"What animals did you see?" Charlie asked.

"A black bear," said Anna calmly. "And lots of other animals, too."

"A bear!" exclaimed Charlie. "Are you sure it was a bear?"

"Of course I'm sure," said Anna.

"I saw a grizzly bear once," said Charlie. "But I've never seen a black bear. You're so lucky. What did it look like?"

"It looked like a giant stuffed animal," answered Anna. "It was sort of cute. And the way he was eating my candy. It was like Winnie-the-Pooh and the honey pot."

"You gave the bear candy!" exclaimed Charlie. "You got that close!"

The Pony Pals laughed.

"He got into my backpack," explained Anna. "I left it on the tree stump. I was over near the corral."

"Anna did drawings of the bear," said Pam.

"While the bear was here?" asked Charlie.

Anna nodded.

"Show him," said Lulu.

Anna opened her pad and handed it to Charlie.

Around 4 a.m. Bear tore backpack.
Ate chocolate chip cookie and candy
with wrapper.

Ponies woke up and scared bear.
Bear made blowing sound and
clicked its teeth. It ran away.

"These drawings are so great," said Charlie.
"I could never do that."

"Me, either," said Lulu.

"How big do you think it was?" asked Charlie.

Anna looked from her drawing over to the
tree stump. "About four times the size of the
tree stump," she said.

"I have an idea," said Lulu as she untied her

shoelace. "We can measure the tree stump with my shoelace. That will help us figure out how big the bear was."

Anna finished her jelly donut while Lulu took off her shoelace. Then the Pony Pals and Charlie went over to the tree stump.

Lulu measured the tree stump. "Write down that it's two-and-a-half shoelaces around," Lulu told Pam. "And one shoelace high. We'll measure my shoelace with a ruler when we get home. Then we'll know how big this stump is."

"Which will tell you how big the bear is," added Charlie.

"Anna, are you sure the bear was about four times the size of the stump?" asked Pam.

"Four times as high," explained Anna. "It was only about twice as wide. I remember thinking that when I was drawing."

Pam wrote down what Anna had said.

"Did you do a map of where your camp site is?" asked Charlie.

"Not yet," said Pam. "But that's a good idea."

"I'll make the map while you break camp," suggested Anna.

"What are you going to do after you break camp?" asked Charlie.

"Why do you want to know?" Lulu asked.

"So you can go tell Tommy and Mike where we are," added Anna.

"I'm not hanging out with those guys today," said Charlie. "This is much more fun."

The Pony Pals exchanged a glance. Should they forgive Charlie for joining with Tommy and Mike to pester them?

Scat

Lulu and Pam agreed that Charlie could hang out with them. They waited to see what Anna thought. She shrugged her shoulders. She didn't care whether Charlie came with them or not—as long as he didn't start bragging again.

"Okay," Pam told Charlie. "You can ride with us today."

Anna sat on the tree stump and made her map. Charlie helped Pam and Lulu clean up the camp site, pack their sleeping bags and supplies, and saddle up the ponies.

When Anna finished the map she met the others at the corral and showed it to them.

CAMPSITE FOR 24-HOUR NATURE WATCH

Badd Brook

Corral

Lean-to

tree stump

Bear leaves

Pine Tree Forest

Charlie looked at the map and then around the camp site. He pointed to an opening between two pine trees. "So the bear went that way," he said. "Did you follow it?"

"We were too busy calming down the ponies," explained Pam. "And it was dark."

"Let's do it now," suggested Lulu. "It would be fun to track him. We'll look for clues—like scat and paw prints."

The four friends went over to the two pine trees.

"Anna and I'll go first and look for tracks," said Lulu.

Anna followed Lulu into the woods. They moved very slowly and looked carefully for clues.

Anna spotted a few strands of black hair on a low tree branch. She showed it to Lulu.

"That's our bear," said Lulu with a grin. Anna went to get Charlie and Pam so they could see it, too.

"Wow," said Charlie. "It's amazing that you found it, Anna. It's just a little bit of hair."

"Lulu's teaching me how to track," Anna told him. "She finds stuff like this all the time."

Lulu took a small plastic bag out of her pocket. She broke off the small branch with the bear hair and put it in the plastic bag.

"How come you had the bag?" asked Charlie.

"I always have them when I'm doing a nature study," Lulu told Charlie. She looked up at Anna and Pam. "I want to track this bear as far as I can."

"Then let's get the ponies and do it," suggested Pam. "When the ponies can't fit, Charlie and I can watch them. That way you and Anna can keep tracking."

"Good plan," agreed Anna.

"You can start tracking now," Charlie told Anna and Lulu. "Pam and I will get the ponies and follow you."

"Blow your whistle if we get too far ahead," Lulu said.

Anna and Lulu went deeper into the woods.

The next clue they found was some bear prints in a patch of mud near the brook.

"Our bear stopped here for water," noted Lulu.

"All that candy made him thirsty," giggled Anna.

They searched the area around the brook for tracks. Anna noticed a crumbling, fallen log. Something had dug a hole under it. She called Lulu over to show her.

"I bet our bear did that," said Lulu. "He must have been looking for insects to eat."

Charlie, Pam and the ponies caught up with them. Charlie brought the ponies to the brook for a drink.

Meanwhile, the girls inspected the area around the log to figure out where the bear went next. There were no clues.

"But he definitely was here," said Lulu. "This log and paw print are evidence."

"We keep calling the bear he," said Pam. "But maybe it's a she and she has cubs."

"Good point," said Anna.

"There are lots of places where he—or she— might have gone back in the woods," said Lulu.

"Let's try different ways the bear could have gone," suggested Anna.

"Okay," Lulu agreed.

"Charlie and I will stay here with the ponies," said Pam.

Anna noticed an opening in a row of bushes. "I'll start there," she told Lulu.

As Anna was walking away from the ponies, Acorn nickered at her as if to say, "Hey, what about me?"

"You can let him follow me," Anna told Charlie.

Charlie put Acorn's reins over the saddle. The pony ran over and nuzzled Anna.

"Acorn thinks he's a detective, too," Anna explained to Charlie.

"He's helped us solve lots of Pony Pal Problems," added Pam.

Anna found a narrow trail into the woods through the bushes. Acorn followed her. After a few minutes, Anna realized that Acorn wasn't right behind her anymore. She turned to find him. "Acorn," she called.

A gentle nicker answered her.

Anna followed the sound and found Acorn sniffing something on the ground. She went over to see what it was.

A glint of silver was the first thing she noticed. Anna wondered if someone had dropped a ring or an earring in the woods. She leant closer to the shiny object. It was a piece of silver foil in a huge piece of scat. Anna called to Lulu.

"Coming," Lulu called back. In a minute she was by Anna's side.

"Look what Acorn found," Anna said. "I think it's bear scat."

"It sure looks like it," said Lulu as she squatted next to the scat. "There are pieces of plants and berries in it, which is what bears eat."

"They also eat candy bars with foil wrapping," said Anna with a giggle.

"That's what that silver is!" exclaimed Lulu. "It's the wrapping from your candy bar. Our bear left this scat. I think we should bring it back to show my dad. It's evidence."

Lulu took out another bag, picked up the

scat with a stick and dropped it in. "Good work, Acorn," said Lulu.

Anna and Lulu followed the bear's trail a little farther. But soon they ran out of clues and couldn't figure out which way to go.

Lulu looked at her watch. "It's ten o'clock," she said. "We said we'd be home by noon. We'd better go."

"We followed our bear pretty far," said Anna.

Anna, Lulu and Acorn made their way back through the woods.

"Wait until you see what Acorn found—" Anna shouted as they came out of the woods. She stopped mid-sentence. Two boys were sitting by the brook with Charlie and Pam— Tommy Rand and Mike Lacey.

Choosing Sides

Charlie, Pam, Tommy and Mike turned when they heard Anna's voice.

"Well, it's the rest of the Pony Pests," shouted Tommy.

"I hate that he's here," Anna mumbled to Lulu as they walked over to the group.

"Did you really see a black bear?" Mike asked Anna.

"Yes," said Anna. "I did. But no thanks to you, Mike Lacey. That was stupid what you did yesterday. Really stupid."

"What's the big deal about seeing a bear?" asked Tommy.

"Have *you* seen one?" Lulu asked him.

"I haven't been looking for any," said Tommy. "If I was, I would."

"Sure you would," Pam mumbled sarcastically.

Anna noticed that Mike kept looking towards the woods. He had a scared look in his eyes. He's afraid, she thought. Afraid he might see a bear. And I saw one, drew it and tracked it. She felt very brave.

"We better hit the trail," Lulu told Pam. "We told my father we'd meet him at the diner at noon."

"Daddy's taking the Pony Pests to lunch," teased Tommy.

"We're meeting him because we're writing an article about our nature watch," Lulu told Tommy. "He's going to get it published."

"Anna is probably the first person in Wiggins to see a black bear," said Pam.

Anna didn't say anything, but she felt proud.

"You're writing about your nature watch for

the newspaper?" asked Charlie in surprise. "I didn't know that."

"We're going to do an article for one of the nature magazines my father writes for," explained Lulu.

"How can *you* write an article?" asked Mike. "You're only like ten years old."

"It's from a kid's point of view," explained Pam. "Not many ten-year-olds do twenty-four-hour nature watches."

"Did you, when you were ten?" asked Anna.

"Gosh, no," said Mike.

"Who'd want to," said Tommy. "It's a dumb thing to do."

Pam ignored Tommy's comment. "I'm sure the newspaper will be interested, too," she said. "They'll probably interview Anna and publish her drawings."

"Big deal," said Tommy.

Mike glanced nervously towards the woods again. "Let's go, Tommy," he said.

"Hey, Charlie," Tommy said. "We're riding our bikes out to this guy's house this afternoon. You can come."

"He has cool videos," added Mike.

"Thanks," said Charlie.

"Let's go," Pam whispered to Lulu and Anna.

The girls went over to their ponies to tighten girths and lower stirrups.

Charlie looked from the Pony Pals to the boys. Anna knew he was trying to decide what to do.

"You can ride on the back of my bike, Charlie," Mike offered. "But let's go. We told Joe we'd, like, you know, be there."

"I have Moondance to ride," Charlie said. "I don't need a bike."

"So you'll ride the horse and we'll ride our bikes," said Mike. "That's cool."

"Are you coming or not?" demanded Tommy.

"I kind of want to hear what Mr. Sanders says about the bear," admitted Charlie. "I'm really interested in animals. You know, because I come from out west."

Tommy laughed, "I'm really interested in animals," he said, mimicking Charlie. "You know, because I come from out west. I guess there are four Pony Pests. Did the girls let you join their club, Sissy?"

"Tommy, you are so dumb," said Pam.

"Tommy, you are so—" Tommy began to say. But he stopped before he called himself dumb. He swung around and reached for his bike.

Charlie put out a hand and grabbed the bike from Tommy.

Anna noticed that Charlie was shorter than Tommy—and smaller—but he wasn't afraid of him.

The Pony Pals mounted their ponies.

"Gimme my bike," Tommy snarled.

"Gimme my bike," said Charlie, mimicking him.

"I mean it," said Tommy. "I'll hit you."

"I mean it," said Charlie and the Pony Pals in unison. "I'll hit you."

Tommy's face was turning an angry red. Mike stood behind Tommy, signaling the girls and Charlie to stop mimicking Tommy. Mike is so afraid of Tommy, thought Anna. It must be awful to be friends with someone you're afraid of.

Moondance whinnied as if to say, "What's going on?"

Anna couldn't help smiling. It was just the sort of thing Acorn would do.

"Ah, take your stupid bike," Charlie told Tommy. "I don't care."

Charlie pushed the bike at Tommy and reached out for Moondance's reins.

"See you guys around," Charlie called out as he mounted his pony.

The Pony Pals and Charlie turned their ponies towards the trail and rode away from Mike and Tommy.

Anna was the first one on the trail, so she was in the lead. As soon as the trail opened up she moved Acorn into a gallop. There was no way that Tommy and Mike could catch them on their mountain bikes. And even if they could, Anna wasn't afraid of them.

She felt the warm saddle beneath her and a nice breeze on her face. She and her small pony had seen a bear. She'd drawn pictures and she had a lot to contribute to the nature article. Anna couldn't wait to tell Mr. Sanders

all about the black bear that she and Acorn saw.

As she rode along the trail, Anna thought about how much she loved being a Pony Pal. And she was glad that she liked Charlie Chase again. But most of all, she loved that Acorn was her pony. She leant forward in the saddle and told him, "Acorn, you're the best."

Acorn whinnied, as if to say, "I know."

Dear Pony Pal:

There are now Pony Pals all over the United States, Australia, New Zealand, Canada, Germany and Norway.

When I first started writing the Pony Pals I thought there would only be six books. Now there are twenty-six books. I am surprised that I have so many stories to tell about Pam, Anna, Lulu and their ponies. They are like real people, who keep having adventures that I want to write down for them.

When I am not writing Pony Pal or CHEER USA books, I like to swim, hike, draw and paint. I also like to visit horse farms and talk to people who love and ride ponies and horses. I don't ride anymore and have never owned my own pony or horse. But my husband and I have two young cats, Lucca and Todi. They are brothers and get along great with our old dog, Willie.

It's wonderful to know that so many Pony Pals from different parts of the world enjoy the adventures of Pam, Anna, Lulu, Lightning, Acorn and Snow White. I think about you when I am writing. A special thankyou to those who have written me letters and sent drawings and photos. I love your drawings of ponies and keep your photos on the wall near my computer. They inspire me to write more Pony Pal stories.

Remember, you don't need a pony to be a Pony Pal.

Happy Reading,

Jeanne Betancourt